To Davis and Avery, my two nephews/dinosaurs
—R.N.

Dedicated to my incredible family, Katrin, Allister,
and the newest little T. rex, Oskar.
—M.L.

DIAL BOOKS FOR YOUNG READERS
Penguin Young Readers Group
An imprint of Penguin Random House LLC
375 Hudson Street, New York, NY 10014

Library of Congress Cataloging-in-Publication Data

Names: North, Ryan, date, author. | Lowery, Mike, date, illustrator.
Title: How to be a T. rex / Ryan North ; illustrated by Mike Lowery.
Description: New York, NY : Dial Books for Young Readers, [2018] | Summary:
Tyrannosaurus Rex enthusiast Sal transforms herself into an uncontrollable T. Rex, partly because her brother said
it would be impossible, but soon discovers the downsides of always being fierce.
Identifiers: LCCN 2017059825 | ISBN 9780399186240 (hardcover) Subjects: | CYAC: Tyrannosaurus rex—Fiction. | Dinosaurs—
Fiction. | Behavior—Fiction. | Brothers and sisters—Fiction. | Assertiveness
(Psychology)—Fiction.
Classification: LCC PZ7.1.N65 How 2018 | DDC [E]—dc23 LC record available at https://lccn.loc.gov/2017059825

Printed in China

1 3 5 7 9 10 8 6 4 2

Design by Jasmin Rubero
Hand lettering by Mike Lowery

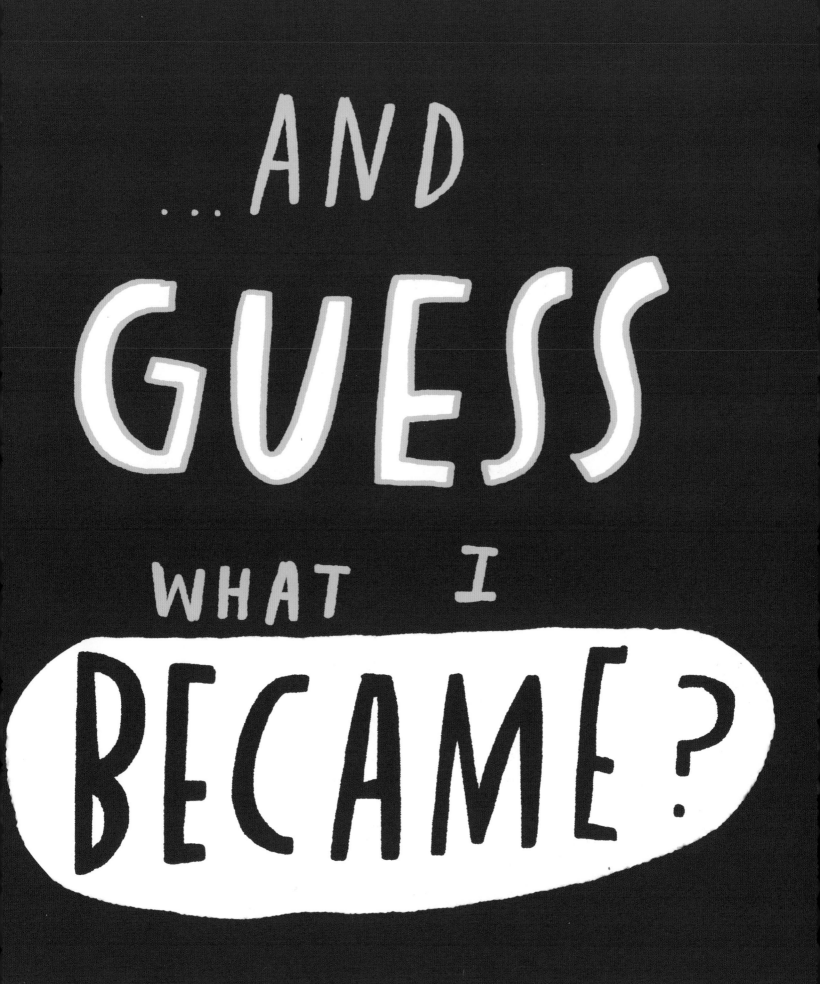

AND SINCE WE'RE ALL FRIENDS HERE I'LL LET YOU IN ON A LITTLE SECRET CALLED

HOW TO BE A

TYRANNOSAURUS REX

IT'S EASY!

STEP ONE:

BE SUPER FIERCE!

GRRR!

STEP TWO:

DON'T BE AFRAID OF ANYTHING!

SPIDER

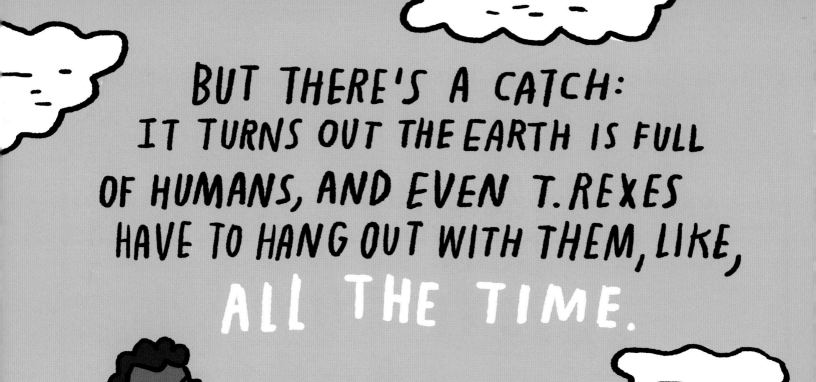

③ THEY GET MAD WHEN YOU AREN'T NICE TO THEM.

BUT WHO EVER HEARD OF A T.REX
THAT CARES ABOUT PEOPLE'S FEELINGS?

NOT ME!!

TURNS OUT THERE ARE OTHER DOWNSIDES TO BEING A DINOSAUR TOO:

① IT'S HARD TO EXPRESS NICE FEELINGS WHEN ALL YOU CAN DO IS ROAR.

② YOUR **DOG** DOESN'T LIKE YOU AS MUCH.

③ DINOSAURS **DON'T WEAR SHOES.** (FUN SOME OF THE TIME, OBVIOUSLY, BUT I DO HAVE SOME **RAD** SNEAKERS I KINDA MISS.)

MY COOL SHOES ↓

WHO WOULD'VE THOUGHT BEING A T. REX WOULD HAVE AS MANY DOWNSIDES AS BEING A HUMAN? THAT'S PRETTY MUCH THE WORST.

IS IT TOO MUCH TO ASK TO BE

100%

AWESOME

100%

OF THE TIME?

HE LAUGHS AT ME, WITH A VOICE THAT HAS NEVER ROARED.
AND POINTS AT ME, WITH FINGERS THAT HAVE NEVER KNOWN CLAWS.
6
AND STICKS HIS FINGERS UP HIS NOSE AT ME, WHICH IT TURNS OUT DOES MAKE YOU LOOK PRETTY SILLY AFTER ALL.
BLAH!

BUT I DON'T MIND BECAUSE HE'S JUST **JEALOUS**: HE HAS TO BE HIM ALL THE TIME.

BUT ME AND MY FRIENDS GET TO BE DINOSAURS...